Andrea

Enchanted Aleutian Princess

Robert Algeri

Author of Alaska Romantic Fiction

PUBLICATION
CONSULTANTS
We Believe In The Power Of Authors

PO Box 221974 Anchorage, Alaska 99522-1974
books@publicationconsultants.com—www.publicationconsultants.com

ISBN Number: 978-1-59433-942-4

eBook ISBN Number: 978-1-59433-943-1

Library of Congress Catalog Card Number:
2020935588

Copyright 2021 Robert Algeri
—Second Edition—

Manufactured in the United States of America

Contents

Alaska 1981

My time frames and time references in these writings are circular, not linear.

When I was younger my mind constantly engaged in new age circular thinking, assigning some symbolic meaning to even the smallest of coincidences. For many years I have been intrigued by thoughts of following my dreams into an unknown land, guided only by mystical spirits calling me home.

The Alaska I was flying into was experiencing a dynamic and exciting period of growth. Oil booms and military buildups coupled with rising gold prices. The Iditarod was gaining popularity along with the Fur Rendezvous Festival. The fishing and tourism industries were expanding as well.

Sullivan arena was about to be built in midtown Anchorage. Anchorage International Airport's air cargo transportation division was entering a rapid and prolonged expansion accompanied by consistent and rising commerce coming through the Port of Anchorage, growth that would peak over the next fifteen years. All this growth brought an increase in populations—more people and more cars.

My wildest dreams never allowed me to imagine the many paths I would travel over the next two years while living in Alaska. Life has a way of taking us in directions we never dream of, and sometimes our reality becomes bigger than the dream itself.

Chapter 1

The Mystery Lady

It's early April 1981 and here I am, flying above the Rocky Mountains north to Alaska. I have been dreaming and fantasizing about coming to Alaska since I was five years old, at eighteen it's finally happening, my dream is about to come true.

As our plane turns north toward the vast blue sky of Canada, we fly over Calgary and Banff National Forest. I am looking down into an amazing, yet menacing wilderness when I start dreaming of northern lights, wolf songs, and Native Alaskan women.

I have always dreamed of meeting an Aleutian princess living in a land full of soaring eagles, schooling salmon, and hungry bears fishing for their survival. I imagine our eyes will meet as she turns her head slightly down to her left, wrist heavy with turquoise bracelet, gold nugget necklace lying against deeply tanned skin.

Our hands slightly touching, we walk along the creek, both silent as we follow the rippling currents that lead us down to the ocean shore, like a dance with nature, we find ourselves stepping over scattered driftwood among the rocks as we go.

A late afternoon sun reflecting off of the rushing water causes hundreds of small rainbow diamonds to bounce like clouds hovering above the water's surface as it flows; the hiss of silt is musical as it embraces us.

The Seat Belt On warning knocks me back into an awake state as our plane starts the descent into Anchorage International Airport. The thought of my dreams leave a warm feeling spreading throughout my chest but the feelings quickly fade as I wake up.

We are passing Valdez off to our starboard, it is barely visible across Prince William Sound. The snowcapped peaks of the Chugach thrust up out of the ocean, white caps on the waves brush against deep blue skies.

The airplane does a big turn over Knik Arm and aligns with the distant runway at Anchorage International Airport. As we drop lower over Cook Inlet, the ice flow becomes more visible—it looks like a giant jigsaw puzzle floating and drifting on the waters.

I start seeing buildings and streets, telephone poles along wire fences that are capped with barbed wire. Below us runway lights are glittering and guiding us home.

In the city I find an array of blue cabs and orange cabs mingled with rising exhaust fumes, truck horns and train horns. Blowing newspapers among scattered trash. My shuttle van turns off of Old International Airport Road onto Jewell Lake Road.

We are driving north toward the merge with Spenard Road, when our van driver starts yelling "All hail good old Joe Spenard, hail ye, hail ye as we hoist a mug, so they say along Spenard, here's to Joe Spenard."

Honestly, I never heard another thing about Joey S the whole time I was in Alaska, never did see the van driver again either. Maybe they got together over a mug and hit it off, did a walkout together and disappeared up into the frontal range of the Chugach mountains.

One thing is for sure, I should have seen this idiotic outburst as a sign of things to come but I just shake my head and laugh to myself. Nowhere am I seeing any sign of pristine creeks, soaring eagles, an Aleutian princess, or even hungry bears.

As we turn at the corner of Spenard Rd and W.36th Ave, I see two ladies lying on the ground next to three guys. The three guys are standing over near a light pole smoking cigarettes and passing a brown paper bag between themselves. We drive past taverns, package stores, pawn shops, and run-down motels with broken lights.

Almost every wood pile is covered with a blue tarp, broken down vans covered with dust sitting in littered parking lots. Most of the cars and trucks I see have cracked windshields, are dirt covered and layered in mud.

The Chugach Mountains are becoming more visible as our drive takes us south onto Lake Otis Parkway. We drive for another half a mile before turning onto East Tudor Road. Mobile homes with full clothes lines come into view, scraggy dogs chained to rusted truck bumpers are loudly barking at crying kids.

As we approach a big bend in the road ahead two guys walk out of the woods and cross the street in front of us, both men are carrying rifles slung across their backs. They look like haggard mountain men returning back to a forgotten civilization.

A tavern with a moss covered roof that has offroad enduro motorcycles parked along a wooden rail comes into view. I see four ladies walking dogs on leashes in front of a Mexican restaurant over on our left. My mind begins to turn things over, picks things apart. Is life accidental, coincidental, or incidental, I ask myself?

A blaring truck horn blasts me back into reality as I realize my dream and perceptions about Alaska and Anchorage have been distorted for all these years. There are no Aleutian princesses strolling along bucolic creeks. I will not be sitting along any beautiful shores with my princess. For the first time in my life I realize I'm not even a prince—my father has never been a king.

As we enter through the front gate of my new home, Fort Richardson, Alaska, my mind begins to create a new dream, a new perception. This time it's going to be based on reality, on what I see and feel in nature, what I hear in the streets of Anchorage.

It's time to put my new dream into action. I want to experience the culture and sounds of Alaska for myself, taste its food, see nature's color, and inhale her scent. I want to feel the land itself if that's possible to accomplish, be a part of her pulse, its inner frequencies.

No matter who I meet, soldier, civilian, resident, or non-resident. Everywhere I go people are telling me, "I've been up here for three years. My girlfriend has been up here for five years." It seems like they will always ask me, "How long you been up from the Lower Forty-Eight?"

I notice they ask it with some hate. They keep telling me I must have come up for the Permanent Fund Dividend or to steal their women, and they say it with a grin.

I keep my Aleutian princess fantasies to myself, but they weigh on my mind. I am constantly scanning any crowd I find myself in, always looking for a friendly face, smiling as she gingerly brushes her flowing hair back. Not tonight in this Thursday night crowd at The Whaler Bar on Muldoon Rd, but there's hope she's out there; maybe tomorrow in another place.

I turn around on my bar stool and the elderly lady sitting next to me casually asks if I can buy her a drink. She introduces herself as The Mystery Lady. She seems fragile and lonely, but her smile is like a magnet, so I agree and buy her a beer.

Mystery lady tells me she can read my spirit and that I am going to find what I came north looking for. I ask her what I am looking for—she smiles back at me, puts a hand on my forearm. Her answer almost blows me out of my seat, I can hear her saying, "Love with an Aleutian princess—it's written in your heart," she explains to me.

Then she says, "Let me share a little Alaskan wisdom with you, my friend. Up here it's all about sharing and taking your turn." She winks, stands up, shakes my hand, and casually walks out the door.

Now ain't that something, I think to myself, all this way and I gotta share. Forget the mystery lady and her Alaskan wisdom.

Chapter 2

Beautiful Fish On 5th

I have seen this girl seven or eight times now over the last two months while we are both walking through Anchorage downtown. She is always smiling and looking up, long brown hair and wearing a cowboy hat that has a curled brim. We have looked each other's way the past several times, smiled at each other, slightly turning toward each other as we pass by.

Now she is coming across W.5th Ave and walking straight toward me with no warning. It's happening real time. I get a little nervous and excited at the same time as she approaches me, but who wouldn't? She is absolutely gorgeous.

She opens with, "Hey it's you."

I respond with, "Wow you're her;" we both smile, now we laugh. We shake hands and she tells me most people call her "Fish."

When I ask her why Fish, she shows me what I think is a unique little fish necklace; I joke we could use it for a fishing lure in a survival situation. "Good colors, gold and silver," I tell her.

She smiles and says, "Nah, never, I'm keeping this one forever my friend."

Then Fish shows me a second little necklace shaped like a fish she is carrying in her pocket; she tells me it's more of an amulet. The amulet is mostly purple with some turquoise and it has a gold chain attached to it; she explains to me that an amulet is an object that protects a person from trouble, from evil happenings.

Fish asks me my name and I tell her they call me "Little Brother" on the street here in Anchorage. Her answer surprises me when she tells me she has heard of me and was glad to finally meet me. She asks me why Little Brother and I tell her I work part time for a guy outside of my military commitment; he owns a lot of different businesses in Anchorage.

He knows a lot of people, I explain to her, and he tells everyone I am like the son he never had. His employees and associates nicknamed me "The Little Brother." I continue to explain that I am very glad he took me under his wing, offered me his guidance as a mentor, and gave me protection from the predators that gaze and prowl along these windy streets.

Fish asks me what I am up to. I tell her I am trying to find out if the lady with the double-decker bus restaurant is parked downtown today. I usually find her somewhere between W.4th Ave and W.6th Ave; I just got done checking out 4th and 5th Aves with no luck, I tell her. She says she could use some food, then asks me if she can come with me to eat.

"Sure thing," I say; we both cross over and take C St down onto W.6th. When we turn the corner onto W.6th Ave we see the bright red double-decker bus parked. This makes us both happy and we smile at each other. She tells me she can't believe the bus is an actual restaurant and I tell her neither can I but it's pretty cool, you are going to enjoy it.

We step into the bus; the downstairs level is full, so after we order our food I have Fish follow me upstairs to the 2nd level seating area. The waitress will bring our food up to us when it's done.

We are both laughing. We find it ironic that the only menu item is fish and chips; we also order clear mugs of hot apple cider with cinnamon sticks for our drinks. This little operation is pretty cool, the owner is also the cook and the waitress.

I ask Fish if she has ever been over to The Monkey Wharf, a local bar, and she says never. I explain the building has a mural of bamboo, fields of grass with palm trees. Let's walk by after we eat for a good laugh, I tell her. Fish explains she has to go to work after we eat but she has some time right now.

"Can we just relax up here and talk while we watch people and traffic out this here window?" she asks me.

"Okay, sure, no problem," I reply.

Fish starts showing me some of her other jewelry, and focuses on an antique wedding ring that, she explains to me, was a family heirloom that got passed down to her—from her great grandmother to her grandmother and now it's with her. It is obviously very important to her. She points out a flower that bridges it all together, smiles at me with a hint of seduction.

As she goes on talking, I can't stop staring at her neck, the way her veins bulge as she talks. Her intensity is intoxicating. Her smile seems like it fills the room, her head is always tilted up as she talks. She gets my blood moving in a very deep warming wave that washes through my body.

I interrupt her, "You seem nervous, do I scare you?"

She asks, "No, why? I ain't scared of anybody Little Brother," she says.

I'm laughing when I tell her she hasn't stopped talking since 5th and C St. Fish tells me it's the opposite, I make her feel safe, she can be free and just talk about herself. She tells me most people only want to talk about themselves, to take things from her but that I was different, I was actually listening to her.

I'm amazed because we have only been together for about twenty-five minutes but I am feeling like I have known her my whole life, like we have met somewhere before. I just can't shake that feeling—her voice has been in my mind echoing, I know the sound of that voice it seems.

She continues talking, telling me she wants to own a jewelry store someday, maybe specialize in antique jewelry. We discuss going out into the Alaskan wilderness together, prospecting for jade and gold she can use to make jewelry; she laughs at the thought of her sluicing for gold nuggets tucked away in a hidden gorge. "Not seeing it," she says, "forget that Little Brother, no way."

I bring her back to what's an obvious trigger point for her when I mention fear again. I ask her, "Aren't you afraid to walk around Anchorage with all that jewelry on?"

Fish gets visibly agitated and tells me "Little Brother, I told you I'm not afraid of anybody, I'm tough, I can take 'em," then she grins and feigns two short punches to my face; I pretend to cover up.

I'm looking at her nodding, a smile starts and we both break out laughing. I ask her what her real name is. "You first," she responds, grinning.

"Nah, not me, you first," I reply, shaking my head to keep the suspense going with her.

I ask her if she has a middle name; her head shakes yes, but she gives me no response.

Fish asks me if I have a middle name, so I shake my head yes. Not talking, we look into each other's eyes, smiling. I am a chess player but, without really thinking, I say "Checkmate."

Fish corrects me and says, "No, it's stalemate," and we both laugh again. By now a few people have come upstairs to eat and they keep looking over at us, so we decide it's time to leave. To be fair, we have been getting louder as time goes on.

I collect all our trash, help her put her black leather jacket back on, and we go downstairs to thank the owner-chef for a great meal—she is always so thankful for my business. She looks at me, then looks at Fish smiling. When she looks back at me I tell her we just met today but we are getting married. Nobody laughs but me—talk about being embarrassed.

Suddenly I feel alone among the crowd, my stomach gets tight and my throat goes dry. I start sweating, or at least I think I can feel sweat beading up on my forehead, when Fish says, "It's okay, let's go now."

She reaches for my hand and leads me outside to the sidewalk. She places both my hands onto her shoulders and pulls me into her closely, looks up at me, and tells me I am a beautiful person, which causes me to blush.

I respond by telling her, "Your beauty intrigues me and I've wanted to meet you for weeks."

Fish is flabbergasted by me saying her beauty is intriguing, but she is also upset that I didn't speak with her a lot sooner. She explains to me that I've been hard to find, and that she was starting to think we would never speak with each other, asks me why I waited.

I want to kiss her but I hesitate at the opportunity, so I end up letting the urge pass by; maybe next time in another place our lips can meet.

Fish and I find ourselves at the intersection of W.6th Ave and A St when it's time for us to part ways. We promise to meet up again, spend more time together. We thank each other for having had a great time today.

Fish hugs me, "Little Brother, next time lunch is on me, okay?" she asks.

"Sounds like a plan to me. I can't wait. Do you have a pencil and paper so you can write down the telephone number to my military unit's barracks?" I ask.

She does have a pencil in a little makeup bag she carries, but no paper. I search my pockets and find a box of wooden matches from The Gaslight Lounge. I remove the outer sleeve, tear it in half so I can write my information down for her. I then explain to Fish how to leave a message properly so that it gets passed on to me.

She tells me to expect a call from her soon—can't wait for us to talk, she says. I am extremely happy about finally meeting her, and she seems to feel the same way about me. Now I will be listening for her voice, and waiting until she calls.

Chapter 3

A Thorny Rose Bush

I stroll out of Club Paris onto W.5th Ave and turn left toward D St. As I'm walking up D St toward W.4th Ave I hear a female voice yelling, "Hey GI, Hey GI." I just keep walking—it's not the voice I am hoping to hear, it's not Fish.

Then I hear her again and this time I decide to turn around. I get immediate lumps in my throat, stunned by her beauty, black hair with a red flower, smiling and waving me toward her. Black eyes shining, smiling, is this her, is this an Aleutian princess, I ask myself.

She has a red rose in her hand, tells me her name is Rose. I think she's joking and she asks me if I am going to card her—do an ID check, as she puts it.

I retort with, "Show me your ID, please." Rose is a nickname for Rosella.

Rose asks me to walk with her, and she will be my tour guide for the night. I find out she grew up in Sitka; she tells me she loves my accent. We get to Resolution

Park around 10:30 p.m. and the night sky is an amazing blue; Sleeping Lady becomes our shining background.

We stop and look up at a statue of Captain James Cook as we enter the park. Rose starts naming all the visible mountain ranges and peaks; she also explains some of her family history, why they moved up into Anchorage from Sitka.

I can't stop staring at her—the tones of her voice, her laugh is intoxicating. She has a way when she jumps up to sit on something that's comical and sensual at the same time—is that my heart pounding, am I short of breath?

We leave Resolution Park and walk across L St over onto W.4th Ave. While we walk toward K St, a car is slowly coming down W.4th approaching us on the other side of the street. As the car slows down even more, the back window is being rolled down.

I can see three tough guys with beards all looking at us when they start yelling, "We getting us a woman tonight. Come on over here. Yea hah." The driver starts revving his engine, the exhaust is making a loud popping sound, he starts spinning the tires, the hot rubber is blowing smoke into the night air.

Rose screams for us to run and starts pulling on my hand, the car blasts down W.4th Ave toward L St and we turn right onto K St running at full speed. We cross W.5th Ave and take a left behind the Voyager Inn, stopping to catch our breath next to a smelly dumpster.

I can hear the popping sound of the rusty exhaust pipe out on W.5th Ave as we jump behind two pickup trucks to hide. Rose is clutching me, crying, shaking her head in despair.

We run across the alley through a parking lot out onto W.6th Ave, hoping we have lost them. Our hearts and minds are racing; we have no weapons on us—unarmed among hungry predators. Maybe this is how a salmon feels as it tries to escape a hungry grizzly bear, I think to myself, always pushing against the current in a chaotic frenzy.

Rose tells me we need to get over near midtown by going through the Delaney Park Strip, but she wants us to run. Thinks maybe we should go back up W.6th Ave to L St, then run down L St to get onto W.9th Ave. We start to run and I follow her, simply because I have no idea where we are going; she becomes my protector.

We finally make it to the Park Strip and find ourselves standing next to an old Alaska Railroad engine. We are hugging as I work my fingers through her hair. She looks up at me, her eyes soaked with tears, her lips an amazing red; we kiss.

Rosella tells me she wants me to walk her home; she gives me an address and asks me if I want to stay with her, to get with her tonight. "2158 Sunset Drive," she says. I repeat it—2158 Sunset Drive, just in case we get split up, she tells me.

Rose motions me with her finger so she can whisper into my ear, and tells me it's almost a three mile walk. We hold hands and start walking in silence across the damp grass over toward W.10th Ave.

The wind starts blowing and at the same time we hear several car horns angrily blowing at each other in the distant. Tires screech behind us and we see an Anchorage police cruiser come barreling around the corner with blue lights on but no siren blasting.

When we finally get to the house, Rose asks me to be quiet as she unlocks the front door. I am starting to relax, feeling comfortable; we survived the mean streets of Anchorage, Alaska, together as a team. We have made it home presumably to hot showers and soft blankets calling out for our tired bodies.

Rose opens the door and as we step in, I can see five guys. Three sitting on a couch, two at a small table playing cards and passing a bottle between them; this is not good.

One of the guys sitting on the couch starts screaming, "What's this, Rose?" Then he yells, "Who is this, Rose?" I hear one of the guys at the table yelling, "Get him." They all jump up at once.

Rose runs into the kitchen and leaves me alone with five angry guys staring down at me. I see her hesitate for a moment while she looks back at me, I can see her look of fear but she also looks sorry at the same time, her black eyes soaked with tears.

I turn and run full blast at an open window that has just the screen down. I put my hands in front of my face, holding my denim jacket up for protection as I dive out of the window, smashing through the screen. As I crash out into the bushes, I can hear the people inside yelling,

"No way . . . did you see that?" I am running fast, I run hard, and I keep running.

Neighbor dogs start barking, pulling against their heavy chains, wet branches are hitting me in the face as I run across yards. I jump over fences and keep running until I find a shed to hide behind, my heart is pounding, my tense body soaked with sweat. I am kneeling in tall wet grass along the shed, my pants are soaking wet.

I look up behind me at distant mountain peaks covered in snow, hoping to see the northern lights dancing above my head, spiritual swaths of energy beckoning me from above.

Instead I see city lights casting pollution, their angry glare hiding the evening skies.

Traffic lights glare all around me, neon signs are shimmering, spot lights circling, sharply piercing evening skies at the nearby military bases. Fighter jets scream as they touch and go, grounds shaking with distant roars.

I cover my ears and close my eyes. My body is getting cold from kneeling in the tall wet grass, I am waiting for a friendly hand to be offered, but tonight it never gets offered.

Chapter 4

Girl Named Mona

It's been two weeks since I met Fish and I still haven't received a phone call from her. I've been downtown Anchorage twice since we met, but I haven't seen her again. One of the times I almost didn't make it back to the base, I got my clothes ripped by the thorns of a rose bush.

It's early September 1981, my roommate Nathan, who grew up in Nenana Alaska, is explaining termination dust to me as we look out our barracks window toward the Chugach Mountain peaks, what we call our backyard.

Suddenly I hear banging on our door and a voice is yelling, "Phone call for The Little Brother." Nathan looks at me with a funny look on his face like, who's the little brother?

I tell him not to worry about it, the call is for me.

I can't believe it, this just may be Fish calling. I run downstairs to answer the phone at the front desk of our reception area. The CQ looks up at me as I approach the desk; he hands me the phone and tells me it's a lady.

"Hello," I say. I get no response and my heart sinks.

I hear a woman saying, "Is this the Little Brother? Hello, Little Brother."

"Yeah Fish, I can't believe you called me but I am stoked that you did, kid," I tell her.

She asks me if I can meet her at the 10–4 Cafe in Mountain View for breakfast the next morning at about 9:45 a.m. but I can't be there, so I ask her to meet me at Burger Jims at 11:30 a.m. and she agrees.

We both say we can't wait to meet up with each other, hang out together again; the CQ shakes his head in disgust as he listens to me gush.

The next morning I am walking up Gambell St from E.3rd Ave toward Burger Jims, I get to the intersection of E.4th Ave and Gambell when I see Fish over at Burger Jims, sitting on a guardrail that divides the parking lots. She stands up and waves. She is not wearing her cowboy hat today but does have her black leather jacket on.

She is wearing a pair of brown suede leather boots that are knee high, they have big laces that run the full length up the back of her calves. Her walk is graceful and smooth, with a small bounce to it. Her head slightly rocks back and forth with each step she takes.

We do a quick hug. I grab her head gently and kiss her forehead. She blushes and smiles up at me. I ask her if she is hungry, and she says, "Yeah, let's eat." Here's a funny thing—Burger Jims serves Chinese food, and that's what we order. Chicken with cashews and white rice—simple, easy, not messy at all.

Fish told me she would pay for our next lunch, and she follows through on the promise. I have to admit, having a beautiful woman buy me lunch in Alaska feels great.

"How you been, kid?" I ask her.

She responds, "Pretty good."

I ask her whether she feels like walking or if we should grab a taxi—we decide to walk.

She asks me to please take her the long way home.

"Where is home?" I ask her.

"Today it's the transit center over off of W.6th Ave. I need to grab the Muldoon bus by 4 p.m." she says.

"No problem, we are about to embark on a major two-and-a-half mile expedition through urban Alaska," I tell her with a smile. Fish is game for the challenge, traversing an urban obstacle course with views included, her friend by her side guiding her.

I jump right into conversation by saying, "Listen, I was thinking of this whole thing about calling you Fish and I would really rather not. What's your name, please?" I ask her.

We take Gambell St to E.3rd Ave and are now heading over to get on Ingra St when she responds by saying, "Last time we talked about middle names, my middle name is Mona. What's yours?"

I respond "No way! My middle name also starts with the letter M—it's Mike."

Mona is laughing, saying, "Really! Mona and Mike." My heart is burning warm, she is getting my blood moving again and I am really liking it.

I respond by saying, "How about M&M? 'M&M Jewelry open for business, Mona speaking.'"

Mona starts saying, "Yeah that's what I'm saying."

We talk about her jewelry store and what it takes to start a business like that, her fears and hopes. Possibly going in as partners, buying a building together, her side a jewelry store and my side a small diner type restaurant.

She asks me why a restaurant. I explain that during high school I went through a food trades program as an exploratory student during my freshman year, then followed that by working at a Portuguese bakery for my last two-and-a-half years of high school.

"Mike the baker," Mona teases.

I retort with, "Yes, and our specialty will be large M&M cookies." She laughs.

We get off N.Ingra St onto E.Ship Creek Ave and follow this to N.Cordova St. E.1st into W.1st up along Christensen Dr. We turn right onto W.2nd Ave then walk all the way until it ends over near the railroad tracks; there's also a trail that runs along the tracks that I like to walk on down by the coast.

Mona has never been here before, and tells me how cool it is to see this part of Anchorage while looking across the mud flats at Sleeping Lady. She wishes she had a camera to capture the moment, freeze it in time, she tells me smiling.

We walk the railroad tracks to Elderberry Park, stopping at the Oscar Anderson House along the way. We both comment on how cool it would be to live here for one full year to experience all the seasons and different people that walk by, spectacular views with fresh air right at your door step.

In Elderberry Park we sit on a small bench for a while and talk about all kinds of subjects. She holds my hand for about five minutes, explaining to me that everyone she meets just wants to take from her, tells me I am not like most other people, I haven't even asked her what she does for work.

She likes this, likes my confidence, likes that I am comfortable not knowing everything. Her words are comforting to me for some reason.

We walk along W.5th Ave until we get to H St, which we cut across to get over onto W.6th Ave. At the transit station we have about twenty minutes before her bus to Muldoon is leaving the station.

She ensures me she will call me again, thinks its best if I didn't get her telephone number right now, she hopes I am okay with that.

I explain to her that's fine, "You called me once, if you do call me again, great, if not I will be very sad," I say with a sigh.

She laughs at me while slapping on my shoulder.

As her bus is rolling away down G St, I am in anguish, wondering if I will ever see her again, will I hear her voice again. This has been one of the most amazing days I have had in Alaska since I came here, and I really just want it to last forever, frozen in time, right here right now.

I have a nagging concern for Mona, afraid that she could walk into harm's way. It gnaws at me, wishing I could protect her but knowing that I can't.

Every time I have asked her if she is afraid to be walking around Anchorage alone, wearing lots of jewelry, with all the cases of missing exotic dancers and girls being kidnapped, I get the same answer from her, "I ain't afraid of anybody, Little Brother. I can take 'em."

I squint up at the sky and can see a huge jetliner thousands of feet above my head, hungry predators running and flying, chasing prey that's filled with fear, the stench of the kill lingering in the air. Somewhere out there monsters are waiting, I can feel their breath.

Chapter 5

Bob Hansen The Owner

It's mid-September, windy and cold but sunny. Today I am walking along the Park Strip on 9th Ave seeing if I can find a small place to buy lunch. I am stopped at B St, thinking I should keep walking until I get to Juneau St, then take Juneau up to E.6th Ave.

I had studied a map over at the People Mover terminal earlier today to get a better idea of how the streets were laid out; I figure if I get to E.6th Ave and can't find lunch, I'll just head back downtown to Club Paris and eat some food there.

When I get to 9th Ave and Cordova St, I can see a cemetery up ahead on my side of the street, lots of nice trees and bushes along fences and stone walls; it's a peaceful stretch of the walk. As I approach Fairbanks St, the Chugach are becoming more visible, I am amazed at being able to look so far ahead—mountain peaks are visible above rooftops and trees.

As I walk across the intersection of W.9th Ave and Hyder St, I start smelling what smells like bread baking, and it reminds me that I am hungry. While in high school, I had worked in a Portuguese bakery back in my home town—we sold pizza slices and sandwiches, so maybe I am in luck in my quest for food today.

I cross the street and am walking up a little hill along a small embankment as the smell is getting stronger. I know I am now close to the source of the smell.

I come up along a small beige cinder block building that has a bakery occupying the corner. As I get to the store front, I can read Hansens Bakery stenciled on the window in bold lettering.

They are offering baked goods fresh daily, donuts and cookies. I also see a "Help Wanted" sign on the window as I walk in. There are two women working behind the counter. Both women look over at me as the bell on the door is announcing my entry.

I am glad to be out of the cold and wind. I ask the woman who approaches me if they sell pizza, and she laughs at me kindly. Ok, no pizza sold here, but they do have donuts. I order two plain donuts to go. As the first woman gets the donuts, the second lady comes over and asks me if there will be anything else for me today.

I tell her, "Yes, I saw your help wanted sign and I am looking for a part-time evening job, I would like to fill out an application if possible and I will buy a carton of milk also." She gets both items and places them on the counter for me.

Both women tell me that the owner of the bakery is away for a few more days on a personal trip, so I should come back in about three to five days and speak with him personally.

I ask them if I can take the application with me so that it's already completed when I return, and they say yes. Okay sweet, donuts, milk, and a job application. I leave knowing I will be back even if it's just to grab cookies and milk on a cold winter's day.

During the week I get the application filled out for the bakery and plan my trip downtown for this coming Saturday. In my experience, Saturday means all hands on deck for a bakery crew. I am thinking the owner will be there, especially after being away from the business for a period of time.

I get excited at the possibility of having a job in an Alaskan bakery and being able to meet new people in the community, interact with the locals.

When Saturday morning arrives I decide not to eat over at our chow hall on base, instead I call a taxi and go for breakfast by myself at the Lucky Wishbone restaurant on E.5th Ave.

After that I figure I can just walk straight down Karluk St to E.9th Ave to get over to Hansens Bakery and drop off this application. I am finding it hard to keep such a small piece of paper from getting damaged. I am wishing I had a folder or an envelope to protect and carry it in, make that a must do.

I love the feel and vibe of Lucky Wishbone—it's a step back in time. It's an extremely mellow atmosphere in here this morning as usual.

The waitress can't believe I don't want coffee; I tell her I would prefer a milkshake this morning, chocolate if possible. I go with a simple breakfast today, two scrambled eggs, rye toast with a side of bacon, and the chocolate malt milkshake of course.

I grab a newspaper from the table next to me and start reading an in-depth story about all the exotic dancers and prostitutes that have been going missing for the last year or so now. This was the big story when I first landed in Alaska—Eklutna Annie and Joanne Messina were all over the news.

I hope nobody I know ever has to experience the breath of the beast coming in for the kill, I tell myself as I read the story. When the waitress comes back and sees the story that I am reading, she says, "That's scary and sad, ya know."

"This is a nasty situation Anchorage is dealing with right now, let's hope they catch this guy as soon as possible," I say.

She agrees but says, "Hey, it's going to be a nice day today right, let's be happy."

I smile back at her, thinking *yes, let's change the subject now.*

After I eat I stand outside on E.5th Ave just watching traffic for a while before I walk across the street. I stay walking on Karluk St and as I am approaching the Karluk

St and E.6th Ave intersection, a great panoramic view of the Chugach mountains appear but you have to be extremely careful in here, cars are driving very fast as they enter a big corner heading out of the downtown area.

I safely cross over and continue down to E.9th Ave. It is a very peaceful walk, a lot of people are waving to me and saying "Good morning." I am amazed at the mountain peaks rippling across the horizon.

I stop in front of a little white cottage style house on E.9th Ave and light up a cigarette. It reminds me of the old New England towns and villages I grew up visiting.

I start going through my mental preparation for a possible job interview, try to get my mind in a talking mood. Being at the Lucky Wishbone has brought me into that food trades mindset as I watched all the staff running around taking care of customers. It's a very busy restaurant for sure.

I can see the bakery is busy from where I am standing. I cross Ingra St over into the parking lot, thinking let's hope the owner is in and can actually find time to speak with me this morning. I really don't want to come back if I can avoid it.

I hold the door open for an older guy coming out and two ladies going in, before I enter. The counter and register area are crowded as I walk in looking around; the smells are amazing.

I see the woman who gave me the job application and I try to get her attention. She looks over at me and holds one finger up, signaling for me to wait while she rings up a customer.

In my mind I am thinking, "Tick tock . . . tick tock are you ready for it . . . tick tock"—it's a mental cadence I use to bring myself into the moment.

The lady waves me over as she wipes her hands on her apron, "I remember you," she says.

I hand her the application saying, "I told you I would come back, is the owner here today?"

The lady tells me I am in luck, that he has been working all night but will probably want to speak with me, so I should wait while she takes my application out back to him.

When she comes back out she asks me if I can wait for about twenty minutes, he will be able to speak with me then. If not, could I come back late afternoon or early evening, because he is interested?

"No problem," I tell her "I can wait for him."

I stand back for a while just watching how the operation flows, watching people's faces as they come in—are they happy, sad—trying to get a sense of the overall feel of the place. I focus on the staff, watching how they interact with their customer base. Is it forced or are they actually enjoying working here?

I finally see a guy coming out from the back area; he pushes through a door while reading my application. He goes over to the lady whom I had spoken with and, as they talk with each other, she points over at me. He looks at me; his head is tilted and he is pushing on the bridge of his glasses. He looks down at my application again.

When I realize he is coming over to me, I walk toward him, extending my hand out. But he walks past me, saying, "Let's go outside." I follow him while we walk out of the building to stand in the parking lot out front. He segregates me away from the door area, and looks back.

The first thing he says to me is, "Why are you here? What's all this about?" He is staring up at me.

I explain my background in food trades and bakery work, how presently I am stationed at Fort Richardson, tell him I had been walking through the neighborhood and stopped in to get donuts, saw his help wanted sign, and decided to apply. I am really hoping to find part-time work in a local business. I have the skills he needs, why not try me out?

He seems to relax when I tell him this, and reaches his hand out to shake my hand. As we shake hands he says, "My name's Bob. I'm the owner here."

I respond, "Nice to meet you. My name's Bob also. Anyone call you Bobby?"

He replies. "No, never, always Bob please, no Bobby ever."

I tell him, "I agree; please call me Bob also.

His biggest concern, he explains, is dependability. He needs me to be there for twenty to twenty-two hours a week, consistently. Bob asks me, "Can you do that for me, Bob?" He starts to fold my application up then puts it into his front pocket, looking at me, waiting for me to respond. I feel like I am being interrogated, and actually I am.

I explain to Bob my biggest obstacle is being deployed out of the area for a field training exercise with my military unit. I could be gone for forty-five days or more at times.

He responds, "No way can that work for me. No, I can't hire you."

I can understand his decision, but I have to try. I tell him, "Please let me work for you for one week for no pay, like an intern. It will be a live interview, and no hard feelings if it's no after that."

Bob doesn't go for it but does tell me, "Listen, if things change for you, if you can give me the hours, come back and leave your name and number with the counter people. Tell them you already met with me, Bob the owner, and I have your application," as he taps his left shirt pocket that has my application in it.

I agree and thank him for meeting with me, for giving me this opportunity to interview with him, possibly come to work for him some day. He gives me a half wave over his shoulder as he walks back inside his bakery, never looking back at me.

Would I really want to work for a guy who keeps referring to himself as "Bob the owner," I am thinking to myself. As I start to walk down E.9th Ave toward Delaney Park Strip, the question to myself becomes—what next?

Chapter 6

The Squirrel

I am standing outside in a misty rain on a military base in Washington state. I was told less than twenty-four hours before departure to be ready to deploy out of the state of Alaska. We didn't receive any more information other than our packing lists and the pickup zone location we were deploying from.

Bob the owner over at Hansens Bakery back in Anchorage made the right decision in not hiring me. I wouldn't even have been able to show up for my first day of work. I had told him I could be deployed for forty-five days or more and here I am, four days after we spoke, in another state for at least forty-five days. Who could have imagined?

I am one of ten combat engineers assigned and attached to an infantry battalion. The 4/23rd from Alaska is doing military operations in urban terrain training for forty-five days down here at Fort Lewis, Washington.

We are informed the battalion totals one thousand fifty-eight soldiers for this operation. Put into perspective, this means one engineer for every one hundred and five infantry soldiers. We engineers are definitely the outsiders on this mission.

We have already been awake doing physical training for the past three hours. It is now 6:10 a.m. and I am in agony, wishing I was back at my home base in Alaska. The grunts are trying to decide if we are going to do an eight mile run or battalion level pugil stick fights. This is not looking good, no matter what they decide they want us to do.

When the command comes down for us to form up, we get marched over into a very large open area. We now stand at parade rest for five minutes, waiting in the wind and rain, just staring straight ahead into the foggy morning. I can hear a chopper overhead in the clouds.

The battalion commander starts screaming orders. He is yelling for everyone to form a large single line circle. The colonel steps over into the middle of the area and yells to form up around him. This is starting to look like a scene from the gladiator era to me.

There is a large pickup truck unloading collegiate football helmets and pugil sticks.

Pugil sticks are twenty pound metal bars wrapped in light padding with thicker swab like padding on the ends. The football helmets have full cage face protection and we also wear hockey style gloves to protect our hands from getting crushed.

An ambulance comes driving out onto the field and parks. The colonel is screaming he wants to see blood this morning, blood guts and gore as he puts it, washed away with all you little babies' tears.

The colonel stands down and lets the executive officer from the infantry call the first fight. He calls for two non-commissioned officers to come forward. They get them geared up with helmets, gloves, and pugil sticks.

They are both E-5's, both infantry, and these guys are tough, ready for the fight. I'm glad they fight on our side, god bless America.

The crowd is stoked, I can feel the energy pulsing through us as we chant, "Kill, kill, kill. Kill, kill, kill," over and over throughout the fight. The ground is shaking as we stomp our feet, fists pumping the air. Today the battle is good.

The executive officer is yelling into a bullhorn as he calls the second fight. Again he is calling for two noncommissioned officers to come forward, both infantry again.

"Kill, kill, kill. Kill, kill, kill. Drive on sergeants, drive on . . . OOORRAA." The ground is shaking again as we stomp our feet. I am hoping I do not get called into the circle today. I am thinking I am crazy for being here, being in the military, for putting myself in this situation to begin with.

After the second fight I can hear the crowd start chanting again, but this time my body goes numb, "Engineer . . . Engineer . . . Engineer," over and over again.

The executive officer calls into the bullhorn, "Engineer against Engineer." Panic sets in.

The battalion erupts into a seething chant "Kill . . . Kill . . . Kill." I am quickly starting to not like being here in the circle at all, what's becoming a circle of fear in my mind.

Let me explain this fear. It's not the fear of the fight, I have had more than ten pugil stick fights in front of five hundred guys or more, I am very skilled at the pugil stick, but this is exactly what causes my fear for me today.

In basic training during our first pugil stick fights at company level, I was tagged with a nickname because of how fast and furious my fighting style was—a fellow soldier Private First Class Nichols gave it to me and it stuck, he named me "The Squirrel."

Nichols was older than all of us at thirty-three years of age during basic; most of the rest of us were eighteen to twenty years old. Nichols was also prior service. We looked up to him as the old buck, but I really had to take it when the drill sergeants started calling me Squirrel also.

Nichols and I came to Alaska together and right away, on day one, he started introducing me to people in the 562nd Engineers as The Squirrel, telling everyone how good of a fighter I am with the pugil sticks. We are both here on this field together and I don't want to disappoint him today if they call my name. Attempt to make him proud of the Squirrel once again.

The executive officer calls over to my squad leader for two names to fight. I hear my name being called first, "Squirrel you're up." Everything starts to move in slow motion as I run out into the center of the circle, my time to shine as they put my helmet on and secure it for me.

"Kill . . . Kill . . . Kill" is echoing loudly now as the infantry battalion get themselves all frenzied out for this fight, whipping themselves up into a nasty homicidal frenzy.

As I look around, every soldier's arms are raised into fists, their faces are contorted into mean and malicious grimaces as they glare. Fists pumping into the air, "Kill . . . Kill . . . Kill" over and over again while stomping their feet.

At the whistle, my fighting partner Specialist Rabitoy jumps toward me with his pugil stick but all I can hear is "Kill . . . Kill . . . Kill" echoing in the background from one thousand voices in unison, a staccato cadence mesmerizing us all into a state of hatred.

We literally pummel each other into the ground. We are fighting on our knees when the battalion erupts into cheers, stomping their feet, shaking the ground beneath us.

I've done it, I've not only survived the circle but have also established my place in it. I can hear the infantry yelling, "Best fight we ever saw, unbelievable battle." They are all red faced, whipped into a frenzy and pounding on each other's backs in hysteria.

As I'm kneeling on the ground recovering from my injuiries, I'm waiting to be called forward again by a voice that never calls me.

Chapter 7

Abracadabra

Mid-November 1981, my bus shudders to a stop in front of Club Paris. People are very scared out here tonight because another dancer, Sherry Morrow, has just gone missing.

Tonight my goal is to locate and find Monica, maybe get her telephone number and establish a line of communication between us, try to have something going with her.

As I get off the bus I can feel the cold in the air. Exhaust fumes hang in the air thickly like fog. Not many people out on the streets tonight, but every bar I walk past is packed with people.

I get over onto W.4th Ave and have to push my way into a small tavern through the crowd at the doorway. The smell of cigarettes and beer is very strong inside the doorway. The smoke is so thick when I first step in that I can hardly see the actual bar area.

Finally, standing over by the juke box, I get a waitress who takes my order. Everywhere I go in Anchorage there is a juke box blaring music. I am looking around when a very beautiful woman comes over and asks me to light her cigarette for her, she tells me her name is Tina.

Tina has shiny black hair almost down to her hips with a tight brown leather jacket on, and there's a belt around her waist that cinches the jacket—it's very sexy.

Tina asks me if I play pool, and starts saying we should team up and play, so how about it, she asks me, "Are you playing with me tonight?"

Glancing down to her left, she is smiling. She waves for me to follow her into the crowd.

I can see the waitress is coming over with my drink, which causes me to lose Tina as she walks away from me. I find a hole at the bar and stand there watching the crowd, when I feel someone pulling on my shirt from behind.

It's Tina and she is yelling into my ear that she wants us to get out of here, "Please, let's just go," she yells over the noise.

"Are you okay? Is anything wrong? I ask.

"No, everything's good. Lets just go." she says smiling.

When we get outside, Tina tells me we have to go find her cousin Elaine, who is up the street at another tavern. We start walking up W.4th Ave into the cold night, neon signs framed with Christmas lights are shining out onto the sidewalk illuminating us.

We can hear loud music coming out of every saloon, pub, and tavern on 4th Ave as we walk. I listen to her talking. Her accent is sensual, she keeps jumping up and down turning to face me. It's very sexy to watch her hair bounce.

An orange cab pulls up and Tina knows the group that gets out from Ambler—they saw Elaine earlier. We cross E St when a car pulls over next to us, Elaine gets out of the car alone. We can hear Steve Miller's song Abracadabra blasting out of the sound system.

The 100,000 Watt Whale radio station is raging in Anchorage tonight when Elaine, Tina, and myself all start singing and dancing to Abracadabra. Dancing in the streets of Anchorage, three people smiling and holding hands, hopefully sharing love with each other.

I can't believe how many people they know, Tina keeps telling me these are "Our people." I am feeling welcomed and it's a very good feeling to have on such a cold night. A small group of about fifteen people are now dancing to Abracadabra.

Elaine has shorter hair that's reddish and is wearing a black leather jacket. She is hugging me and nudging her face into my neck, coaxing me to respond. Elaine is telling me I am beautiful and how much she loves my east coast accent, asking me if I "Want to get with her and Tina tonight?"

Tina is laughing telling us, let's get out of here and go to my place. She yells at a cab and the driver starts beeping as he pulls over for us. I hear her telling him, "Down by Abbott and Lake Otis." I have no idea where that area is.

We are all sitting in the back of the taxi laughing and hugging, we start kissing back and forth between Tina and me, then Elaine and me. It's getting intense when the cab driver starts yelling at us to calm down back there.

This causes us to all laugh, while Elaine pulls a bottle out of her pocket book.

It takes about twenty minutes but we get to a very nice home. I follow both ladies from the cab through the front door.

As I'm turning around from shutting the front door, I feel something hit me in the head very hard. I look up from the ground, and a woman I have never seen is standing over me with both hands raised above her head, holding a frying pan.

She starts screaming and swings the pan down at me again. My palms catch most of the blow, the floor absorbs the rest.

I'm able to get up and instinctively I chase her down a hallway but she slams a door in my face and locks it. I start knocking loudly asking her why she attacked me.

I am walking back to the living room, yelling for Tina and Elaine. My heart is pounding. I hear a voice coming from the kitchen area, where I find Tina sitting on a chair at a table.

She has her head tilted back and is chanting, pounding the table with her left hand while she chants. She looks at me but it seems like she is looking past me, when I feel another hard hit on my head. Elaine has a shoe in her hand and is hammering down at me, screaming I scared her cousin Teresa, why did I have to be so mean?

Teresa must be the lady who hit me with the frying pan. At this point I wasn't understanding how I scared someone who almost crushed my skull. Not a great first impression of Teresa, and now she seems to have turned her older cousin against me.

The tides have turned, a tsunami of emotions wash over me, drama ensues among the chaos.

I wake up in bed the next morning with all three women lying on me or partially on me. I can't remember what happened for the most part, but getting hit with a shoe multiple times is coming back to me.

Thinking I must have got knocked out, I am thankful to be breathing, three smiling women touching, rubbing on my aching body. I have an uneasy feeling though, that these three ladies actually attacked me last night, and now we are lying around like four great friends.

Seduce and attack seems to be the game up here in Alaska.

Tina tells me I must feel like I am "in heaven being in bed with three ladies." All three ladies smile at once.

I can smell and hear bacon cooking, so I ask them, "If all of you are in here with me, who is cooking out there in the kitchen?"

Tina just told me her husband Don was cooking us all breakfast. He's a great cook, she says. I jump up and start getting my shirt on while the girls are laughing. Her husband, huh, please no, not Don the husband.

My head is clearing as I realize my actual situation. I am hungover, I got beat up by three women wielding domestic tools of destruction. Now one of the ladies' husbands is in the other room cooking us all breakfast, a guy named Don, and Don's a great cook I am told.

I don't remember if there was any intimacy other than kissing, but it's still not looking good for me at this point. I mean this guy has to be pretty upset. I am in his master bedroom lying in bed with his wife and her two cousins.

It's obvious I have been here all night. Nothing in my life to this point has prepared me for this turn of events. Damn, what am I doing here like this? Okay, stay calm, if he was going to kill me I'd probably be dead by now.

I walk out into the kitchen. Don is wearing an apron and standing at the stove, cooking. He turns around and asks me if I eat toast.

"Sure, rye if you have it," I say.

By this time Tina, Elaine, and Teresa are out in the kitchen with us and everyone acts like nothing ever happened, nothing to see here, people, so please move along.

Don never speaks to any of us other than asking what food we want. When he gets his own food, he takes it into the living room and eats alone, in silence, staring at a television that isn't turned on.

Several hours later, we pull up to the front gate of Fort Richardson and I show my military ID to the MPs at the guard house, they wave us through. We pull up to Building #664 and the car stops. Tina's husband, Don, had just driven me thirteen miles in total silence.

As I get out of the car, I lean back in to tell him thank you when he screams "GET LOST" at the top of his lungs. He puts his car in gear and stomps on the gas pedal. I quickly jump back out of the way as he spins the tires, spitting gravel against my shins.

I turn around to stare at the Chugach Mountains. I can see the snow being blown off the peaks into small wispy clouds. I start dreaming about being on the go and coming down that mountainside. I'll be looking for a friend but what will I find?

I'm dreaming I can see a woman standing in the background waiting for me to find her. She's waiting for me to come to her in the middle of the night, seduced by the beat of her heart.

Chapter 8

Her Name Is Andrea

My unit deploys tomorrow for my first major winter training exercise. It's been on our schedule for two months now so the date is ingrained in my mind—Monday, November 30, 1981, we fly north on C-130s at 0530 hours out of Elmendorf AFB.

This is what I came to Alaska for from a military perspective—being immersed into wilderness for the first time, hundreds of miles from society, with just the gear and each other, squad to platoon.

Saturday morning the CQ on duty gave me a message that came in late Friday evening for me, it was time stamped at 11:22 p.m. and it was from Mona.

My heart bounces, my blood is moving as I read her message, "Try to be downtown on 4th or 5th Ave this Sunday morning between 9:45 a.m. to about 12:00 noon, hope to catch you there, mona/fish."

Being downtown Anchorage early Sunday mornings is one of my favorite times to be there, I enjoy the solitude while walking, especially down on the trail that runs along the railroad tracks. The views out over the mud flats across Cook Inlet toward the southern reaches of the Alaskan mountain range are spectacular.

Today as I look out over the water, Sleeping Lady is reminding me of a love that hasn't been found yet. Her melancholic serenity wraps its arms around me as I walk. Is there really anyone that can hold us tight in life, I wonder, or is it an illusion?

I would love to bump into Mona. I am in anguish not knowing whether we will connect today or not. I need to hear her friendly voice, her soothing tones of seduction.

It's 9:05 a.m. when I decide to wander up off the waterfront, meandering through Anchorage on this lovely Sunday morning, try to find some food to eat, maybe somewhere I haven't tried yet, someplace new to me.

I stay walking on 4th Ave, alternating walking on both sides of the street, when I decide to walk into the Army Navy Store and look around for about ten minutes. I come out and walk past a lot of small bars and groups of people already gathering on corners.

I cross over to look at a statue of Atlas holding up the world on top of the Fur Factory building, when I see a small diner called White Spot Cafe right next door.

Not sure if I noticed this place before, so I decide to check out their food this morning. I like the little booth style tables, so I tuck into one of them instead of sitting up at the counter. I see what I want right away on the menu. I am going with the reindeer sausage omelet today, and chocolate milk or tomato juice, maybe both.

I have a small glimpse past the counter area out onto W.4th Ave and, as I am waiting for my food, I see a familiar person walking past on the other side of the street.

It's her, that's Mona who just walked by. I jump up and tell the counter girl I will be right back. I run out the door and cannonball across the street in a full run, almost getting hit by a car. When the tires screech, people turn to look, including Mona.

I see her put her hand up to her mouth, then start waving. When she realizes I am okay, she smiles. There it is—that sky wide smile, deep brown eyes, tilted head; yes, it's her again.

She has a pair of brown suede leather boots on. They are knee high, with big laces that run the full length up the back of her calves, sensual and casual.

"Hey, I'm about to eat. Can you join me?" I ask.

She replies, "For sure, but be careful next time crossing the street," with a huge grin. We both laugh but I am kind of embarrassed.

Stumbling and bumbling across W.4th Ave at 10:15 a.m. on a Sunday morning isn't the greatest way to impress anybody, especially the woman you are having feelings for, but it seems to have worked for me today. Maybe the love gods have answered my prayers.

When we get back inside the White Spot Cafe, my food has just arrived. As we start to sit down, Mona's voice brings me back into the moment. I hear her asking me if I am ready to exchange real names. I am surprised but pleased.

"Yeah, but do you need food? Let me get a second dish and you can split mine with me." She agrees. We get our waitress to bring a second plate and set of silverware for her. I tell the waitress I will tip her good.

She smiles and says, "Thanks, honey, I need it."

"Coffee? Yes, bring it on please, at your convenience ma'am, thank you very much," I say.

I look at "Mona" and say "So." She responds, "So."

"Ok then, my name is Bob, Bob Algeri."

She starts saying, "No way, no way . . . Algeri, . . . my name is Andrea Altiery, they are spelled similar. Are you kidding me?" Andrea asks.

I'm going, "No way Altiery, we both have the same middle initials, the same last initials," I hesitate but then joke with her, "Listen, if we get married you will have the same initials, no changes, your last name will sound similar and you have a wedding band already. Personally, I think it's meant to be," I explain to her.

Andrea starts laughing, saying, "We may never know, we may never know . . .," staring at me, smiling with that huge smile. Her eyes penetrate into my heart.

"Why didn't you wear your cowboy hat today?" I ask.

She explains it went missing at work one night last week. Then Andrea asks me, "Why, can't we get married if I don't have that hat?"

"Is that a proposal, young lady?"

Our waitress interrupts us with more coffee but I feel a sense of relief because the distraction gets us off the subject of marriage for a while. Don't want to scare this girl or myself with too much marriage talk this morning.

Andrea starts talking about her jewelry store; she thinks she has found a location in midtown over by 15th Ave and Eagle St, and asks me if I still want to be in with her.

This reminds me about having submitted my application to the bakery, I tell her about it and she says she knows where that place is. I explain how the job will never work out but at least I am walking into more food businesses in Alaska seeing how they do it up here.

"We will have a jewelry store and restaurant combination someday, I promise you, in midtown Anchorage, right here in Alaska, kid," I promise her.

She responds by slapping me on my shoulder while grinning at me.

After we eat we decide to take a walk, Andrea asks me if I have any good bud on me to get her high with, I tell her yes, and you're going to enjoy this. I have her follow me back up E.4th Ave to Barrow St. I explain there's a great spot near the A St overpass area where we can sit and smoke—it's called Barrow Park.

I have sat there many times, usually alone at night watching the railyard area swim in light, listening to its sounds in the distance. Andrea talks about loving the waterfront, being by the sea, surrounded by ocean blue.

When we get over into Barrow Park there is nobody there. We walk along the upper tree line and find a great place to sit. There's not much snow, but we kick it back to clear an area. We find soft grass just below. I have a windbreaker that we lay on the ground and it protects us from getting wet.

Our conversation is flowing great, Andrea can't understand why someone like me enlisted in the military, explains to me that I just don't seem like the military type. I agree with her and tell her I am one and done, no reenlisting for me. I want to be wild, I tell her, wild and free.

Andrea brings up our last name similarities again, and says she just realized we share five common letters in our last name. A pentagram, she explains, is a five-pointed star, symbolic of white magic to many cultures.

We both just stare out over the rail yards and Ship Creek area in silence. We both tilt our heads and glance at each other sideways, then quickly turn away smiling.

All of a sudden Andrea does a sitting hop and bounce to face me. She crosses her legs and places her elbows onto her knees leaning in toward me, and asks me, "Bob would you seriously consider marrying someone like me? You don't even know what I do, where I live, I mean . . ."

"What do you mean, Andrea, I don't care what you do or don't do. Be happy, be yourself. My biggest concern is you constantly putting yourself in danger, walking into a trap, getting yourself robbed or worse out here."

I bring up Sherry Morrow, a dancer who went missing out of the Wild Cherry just two weeks ago. It's been headline news. Andrea tells me she actually knew her and really hopes she is alright but that she probably just moved as part of the circuit. She explains the circuit to me and I nod.

"Listen, please be on full alert out here, Andrea, at all times, night and day." She calls me "Little Brother," gives me a cold glare.

"Little Brother, I ain't afraid of anybody, nobody, that's it," she shakes her head in dismay, gets a little sad. My heart drops because the last thing I want to do is bruise her emotionally, hurt her pride, destroy her confidence.

I tell her, "I know you're tough, I believe you can hold your own. I just need you to know I am very concerned for you out here, Andrea."

I remind her that infrastructure and perimeter security are an integral part of my job with the military. I continue to explain that we are always being advised from the chain of command to stay safe out here. It's just in my nature to reciprocate. I tend to get a little paranoid at times.

She nods in understanding. We both smile and relax again.

I tell her I have to leave the next day for about seventy-five days, going north for advanced weapons training in Arctic conditions, I will be back mid-February.

"Wow just in time for Valentine's Day" both of us respond together, while tenderly pushing the palms of our right hands together.

I ask her if she will be waiting for me or will forget me by then. Andrea laughs and says, "No way am I forgetting about you anytime soon, Little Brother, you're in my mind," as she taps her forehead, grinning at me.

What Andrea tells me next hits me like a wrecking ball.

She starts telling me she is doing a photo shoot in four days for a guy over in midtown, and that he is going to pay her $300. I snap my head in her direction saying, "What did you just say Andrea?"

"What?"

"Haven't you been listening to me or the rumors on the streets Andrea? All the girls are scared saying this guy might be the killer, nobody can understand why the police haven't grabbed him yet for questioning, Andrea."

Andrea looks at me for about ten seconds in silence before breaking out into a hysterical laugh. She says to me, "Bob, this guy is scrawny. He couldn't harm anybody. Believe me, it's legit."

To prove her point she follows with, "Listen, I'll save some of the money I make and when you get back lunch is on me, any place in Anchorage on me."

I rub my head, shake my head, just let it go, I'm telling myself. I can't let it go so I try one last thing. I say to Andrea, "Andrea if I pay you $300 to not do the photo shoot, and if I buy you lunch anyplace in Anchorage when I get back, will that keep you from doing it?"

She responds teasingly and with a huge smile, "What would keep me from grabbing your $300, then going to do the photo shoot and grabbing another $300 without you ever knowing?"

Andrea is grinning and I just can't resist so I retort, "Ok, I will pay you $600 and buy you lunch anyplace in Anchorage if you just agree to not do anything but wait for me to get back. Deal, just wait for me to get back," my hand is extended out to shake but she doesn't grab it.

I can tell she has made up her mind, and all I can do at this point is wish her luck, respect her decisions. Andrea and I both seem to be caught up in a maze of emotional chaos right now—emotions, feelings, and desires leading us both astray.

In my mind I slip into a dream. I am standing in the background watching her as she walks down that lonely road. I can see her waiting for a shadow, when she turns around and sees it coming toward her, it's already creeping in to keep her.

Chapter 9

Positive Vibes At The Coastal Trail

A ndrea, check this out. Look at how the light is being reflected off of the swirling snow dancing around Sleeping Lady's head," I whisper.

"Sweet. That's riveting. I love the entourage of colors," Andrea whispers back.

Andrea reaches for my hand, and we entwine our fingers together while alone gulls forlorn cry echoes off of the choppy surf roiling against the rocks below us.

As we continue to meander along the coastal trail inviting shadows splash across our path. Andrea abruptly stops walking and pulls me tightly into her, snuggling her head against my chest. She lets out a long sigh.

"Is everything good?" I ask.

She turns her head and looks up at me, "I want us to have something together. I want to spend more time with you."

"I like the sounds of this," I reply.

Andrea continues, "My future is up in the air. I want to open an antique jewelry store, but I am not sure if I should return to Hawaii or launch right here in Anchorage."

"What's your gut feeling?" I ask her.

"I think being here in Alaska could work out for me, but I am reluctant to give it a go on my own," she says.

"I can understand your concerns. Doing business up here is expensive, and you have to deal with a major boom or bust mentality," I reply.

"In Hawaii, my business would be more consistent on a year-round basis. We have a longer tourism season on the islands," she explains.

"You have a lot to think about, that's for sure," I reply.

"Are you seriously thinking of owning a business?" Andrea asks me.

"No, not really. At one point in time, I was thinking of opening a small deli or bakery, but those thoughts have evaporated from my mind," I reply.

Andrea responds, "People like you. I feel you would do well with your own business."

"Thank you. Duly noted, I appreciate all your positive vibes," I reply. At the time, I didn't realize I would never speak with Andrea again. Looking back, I wish I had said more.

Chapter 10

Has Anyone Seen Andrea

February 17, 1982, my sortie has just landed at Elmendorf AFB. We are returning from an extremely physical period of training that was also amazingly beautiful.

Fresh Alaskan powder at eighty-five miles an hour on a single ski bombardier snow machine, this is pure pleasure. Snowshoes and Nordic traverses, crampons, and ice axes—over the edge we go.

When I get to my barracks, I immediately check in with the daytime CQ inquiring about messages, and I am told I have zero messages. Nothing came in for me, I am told. I am going to keep checking back over the next few days. Sometimes messages get misplaced.

I will be going downtown Anchorage within two to three days anyway, so I can walk around and try to find Andrea, but I am really starting to wish I had asked her where she works. Maybe if I had pushed harder to get her telephone number we would be talking right now instead of all this mental wondering.

My mind has been occupied with thoughts of Andrea Altiery pretty much the whole seventy-nine days I have been deployed up north. I can't wait to have lunch with her at Club Paris, walk with her down by the waterfront, and tell her I missed her.

Hold her hand while I listen to her voice, follow her gaze toward the horizon as we walk. I need to find out if Andrea is feeling the same way, if she really wants to have something going between us or not, last we spoke she was into it.

I came to Alaska so I could experience wilderness, yet the whole time I was deployed up north I couldn't wait to get back to urban Alaska. I had grown up thinking the call of the wild was supposed to beckon me into a remote and isolated location. Now that I have found it, it's calling me back to Anchorage, looking for a woman with a smile and a plan.

I can see her walking with brown suede leather cowboy boots on, the ones with the big laces that run up the back of her calves, that black leather jacket shining in the midnight sun.

Saturday, February 20, 1982, I find myself walking around Anchorage looking for Andrea. Everyplace I go into, I ask them if they know Fish, but nobody seems to be able to help me.

I continue to wander up and down 3rd Ave, 4th Ave, 5th Ave. It seems like an eternity.

I walk on every side street and into every alley I come across, until I find myself over at Resolution Park, in the shadows of the big lady again, the one known to the locals as Sleeping Lady.

I am sitting on one of the lower levels of Resolution Park, looking out across Cook Inlet toward the Sleeping Lady. Today it seems like this girl mimics me, laughs my way as she casually gazes up at the night sky.

I feel torn and overcome with anguish as I stare down at the mud. I can hear voices laughing as people walk below me on the railroad tracks, gulls gliding above my head talking to each other with forlorn cries.

It's a sad walk for me over to the transit station so I can catch a bus. As I am walking, my thoughts drift to Andrea again one more time. I am starting to think she has left Alaska and danced on, as they say.

I am wishing her well, sending out positive vibes along the waters, smiling that I knew her from the little glimpse she has allowed me. I really do hope she gets that jewelry store someday.

I find myself staring at the long row of pay phones inside the bus station, when I realize I might be waiting to hear her voice from a phone call that will never come.

Chapter 11

Slithering Snake in A Tree

Four guys from the base, and I, are at the Wild Cherry tonight, watching undressed and scantily clad women jumping around to all kinds of music. When I say jumping, that's what I mean—not much real dancing happening at the Cherry, but it's erotic and sensual.

As usual, I am keeping an eye out for Andrea. I still haven't given up hope. I would rather be out there someplace with Andrea than in here. I need to get out and walk around, meander through Anchorage looking for a swan.

I decide to break off from the group and take a walk by myself through downtown. I step out onto the sidewalk and start walking up E.4th toward W.4th Ave.

When I get to the intersection of E.4th Ave and A St, the traffic is pretty heavy, so I have to wait for the cars to clear before attempting to run across the street.

Just as I am getting over onto W.4th Ave, a taxi pulls up in front of a small building about seventy-five in front of me. I keep walking along the sidewalk approaching the taxi, when an extremely beautiful woman comes walking out of the building.

I can't believe how white her blonde hair looks against the black denim jacket she is wearing. She has sexy red ear muffs on. She starts smiling at me and yells, "Hey, you."

I start looking around to make sure she is speaking to me, which causes her to laugh. "I really think I am going to like you," she is saying. Before I can say anything, she tells me her name is Annie, and if I was a smart guy I would get in and go with her. Get into the taxi, she says.

I jump in and introduce myself to her as Little Brother. We shake hands. She yells up to the driver, asks him to pull over real quick so she can run into a nearby package store and grab us a bottle.

Annie gets back into the taxi and asks me if I like cognac while she's cracking the seal. Gives the driver some address off of L St. It's nearby, she tells him. After a few sips, she jumps over onto me and starts kissing my neck, kissing my ears, grabs me by the head telling me I am all her's tonight.

I am in total disbelief at this point, frantically trying to get my mind into the game that's unfolding very quickly and unexpectedly during this taxi ride. I was out looking for Andrea and now I find myself being mauled by Annie. Anchorage, Alaska, is crazy, man.

When we get to her place, it gets pretty steamy between us as we start kissing and drinking while walking down the hallway, the cognac is starting to warm us up pretty good.

We walk into a really nice place with a small picture window looking down at L St. Annie tells me to put music on while she hits the shower, asks me to relax and take my shoes off, grab a beer if I want one, "I will be back to play with you, I promise," she tells me.

She has a nice stereo system and quite a music collection. I choose some west coast jazz, put it on the turntable and start to look around her living room. I am looking out at this great view of the night lights of Anchorage when I see a person behind me being reflected in the window—a person that's not Annie.

Is that a guy, no way, she never mentioned another guy. Here we go again, what's this now?

I turn around and yes, it's a guy. He's dressed in a long black nightgown that's hanging open, he is wearing teal blue shorts underneath, and on his feet are white slippers. He has long hair that is thinning with a scraggy beard.

I ask him, "Where is Annie?"

He starts laughing at the question and begins walking toward me, wrapping a long feathered scarf around his neck, telling me it's his "pet boa named Charlie." The guy is telling me, "You are so pretty . . . so pretty," while pointing at me.

He stops and leans on a column in the middle of the living room, flips the last foot of the scarf around his neck, looks at me, and asks, "We gonna do this, good looking?"

"No, I'm good with that stuff man," I tell him.

I start backing up away from the guy to grab my shoes and jacket, when I trip. As I am falling, I land on a glass table, which completely shatters under my body weight. Luckily I avoid being cut but I do have glass stuck to both the palms of my hands.

I forget about my shoes and jacket, I just get up and run, aiming to get out the door.

Once out of the suite, I stumble to a staircase and find myself running down three stairs at a time until I get to the ground floor. I crash against the exit door.

When I make it outside, I immediately realize I am not wearing any jacket or shoes. Luckily, though, I am wearing a thick pair of wool socks, which help protect my feet as I run up the street on the cold pavement.

I have to stop and lean on my knees to catch my breath; my heart and mind are racing, it feels like my heart is going to burst through my sternum any second now. I realize I am shivering and really need to grab a taxi before I freeze to death right in downtown.

There are two street signs on the light pole at the corner where I am standing—one says L St, the other one says W.6th Ave. I am totally speechless. No words can describe what I just went through in my mind other than insanity, insanity over and over again going through my mind, total insanity in Anchorage, Alaska, tonight, my friends.

I cross over onto W.6th Ave and start walking, crushed again, just like the glass table that shattered back up in Annie's suite—Annie and Charlie the boa sitting in a tree.

My mind gets knocked back into reality when I hear a lady screaming from a car parked up in front of me. As

I walk slowly toward the car I can hear her screaming, "Help me, he's raping me, help me, he's raping me."

I look into the car and see a lady lying in the driver's seat area. There's a guy lying on top of her trying to pull her dress up around her waist. He has it fairly high up her thigh already, the black lace of her undies is showing on her hip. The lady sees me looking in at her and starts screaming for me to get him off her—please help me.

She has long bushy red hair. I can see the fear in her eyes. She looks absolutely petrified.

So I open the passenger door and start pulling on the guy's legs while yelling at him, "Let's go; get out, leave her alone, get out." He starts kicking at me. He lands a solid kick on my chest, then follows me out of the car as I jump back away from him.

I recover quickly as he tries to slam a big right fist against the left side of my head. As we both start punching, he slips and falls against a parking meter. He looks up at me while putting his hands in front of his face, shaking his head back and forth, "No, no," he says.

I turn to see if the lady is going to be okay, when she starts running around the car screaming at me that I hurt her husband. When the lady gets to me, she starts swinging her pocket book while screaming at me, "Why did you hurt my husband? I'll kill you . . . I'll kill you. I hate you . . . I hate you, I hate you." She spits in my face.

No time to psychoanalyze, so I break contact with both of them and start running up W.6th Ave. I have run about seventy-five feet when a taxi pulls over in front of me. The driver is yelling at me, trying to get my attention, I stop and lean into the open window.

The driver is asking me if I need help getting out of here. I yell, "For sure" and jump in. I ask him to get me to Fort Richardson as quickly as possible. I will tip you very good, I tell him. He's nodding approvingly.

The driver is asking me if I know those people. I reply to him jokingly that I don't even know if I know myself anymore. I hear you, my friend, he replies. Finding yourself can be a very long journey, he starts to explain with a serious demeanor, which I appreciate.

I decide to interrupt him and explain, "I think finding yourself and knowing yourself are the same thing and if you have never left yourself then what is there to find, my friend?"

I continue to explain, "It's like finding god, man. If he lives within me like all the religions teach, why would I spend time looking for him?"

I turn to look out the window reflecting on my life's insanities. In the background I can hear the taxi driver saying, "That's deep, man, that's really deep."

Chapter 12

The Search Goes On

I am sitting in the transit station hoping to catch a glimpse of Andrea. Maybe she came back into town and we can have a serendipitous moment between us. Maybe Andrea found out I have been looking for her and now she is avoiding me—this can drive any guy insane, not knowing.

I am already over by W.6th Ave and C St so I decide to go into The Monkey Wharf, take in a different scene than I usually do, maybe meet some new faces tonight, grab a couple shots of whiskey before moving on through town.

As I step inside the door, I bump into two guys I know from the base. They are glad to see me, they start telling me the crowd is a little hostile toward the military in here, good to have some back up tonight. I explain that tonight I am not anybody's back up. You guys are on your own, I tell them. "Be safe," I say, as I am walking away from them, shaking my head.

Backup, backup, I am not doing any dirty work tonight if I can help it, I need to relax and heal, maybe find some new friends. I don't represent the military out here at all, it's all about me tonight.

Where's the military if I need help right now? Are they buying me a hotel tonight? I don't see a sign for the chow hall anywhere. CID can kiss my hams for fists, knees to the forehead; stand down, my man.

As I finish my mental rant, I see a woman walking toward me pouting, sultry red lips with black hair down past her hips sipping her drink from a straw. She is wearing a very sexy yellow blouse and doesn't waste any time introducing herself to me.

She shakes my hand and says to me, "Hi, I'm Jeanette. Can we get out of here?"

"Absolutely, I was hoping you would ask, let's go," I reply.

When we walk outside, Jeanette turns around and grabs me by my shoulders, pulls me into her tightly, asks me if I think I can handle her tonight, coyly looking up at me smiling. She reaches down and grabs me, pouting with those sultry red lips again. Her fleece jacket feels like a wild animal's fur in my hands.

I ask Jeanette if we need to grab a taxi and she says no, that her car is parked around the side of the building, would I mind driving for her?

"No, no problem I can drive," I reply.

We get around the corner and she walks over to a beautiful black Corvette Stingray and I honestly think she is kidding with me, cranking the old shaft to get a laugh, I am thinking to myself.

No, not kidding, this is her car, the keys in her hand just opened the door, wow no way, I start kidding with her, "Jeanette with the Vette, are you kidding me?" I ask her.

Jeanette is smiling, telling me to jump in, "It's cold out here," she throws me the keys.

Before I start the car, I look at her and say one more time, "Jeanette owns a Vette, no way will anybody ever believe this," I tell her.

She jumps over and kisses me, then says, "Gentleman don't kiss and tell. Now let's get outta here, okay?"

I ask Jeanette where we are going and she tells me we are going to take C St all the way down to W.36th Ave, then W.36th Ave to Wyoming Dr "Just drive I will guide you." She opens her pocket book and pulls out a small bottle, passes it over after she drinks half and I guzzle the rest.

I have been a passenger in a Corvette but I have never driven one until now. This beast is tough to keep straight on the icy roads even with great tires on it. As we approach the intersection of C St and W.Northern Lights Blvd, the light changes very quickly.

I use too much brake while down shifting. We spin across the intersection doing three complete three hundred and sixty degree spins before we slam into a snow bank. The car stops with the nose up on the snow bank like a ramp pointing us up toward the sky.

I look at Jeanette, "Did I tell you I don't have a license?"

She looks at me and starts laughing, saying, "Wow, like I couldn't tell. Where did you learn to drive . . . oh that's right, the guy driving my car forgot to tell me he has no license," with a huge smile; she stays calm.

Luckily there were no cars around, no police around, we started to feel alone looking up at the night sky through that little Corvette's windshield, star-studded sky twinkling above us.

We are able to gently back the car down off the banking out onto C St. Everything seems to be in order, we don't see any damage as we walk around the car checking it out. We lucked out in a really big way, we both agree.

I ask Jeanette to drive and she gladly takes the keys from me, gets us going back in the right direction. I am embarrassed she can drive this car like an expert, up and down the gears smoothly, using engine speed only to slow us down around corners. I like her technique.

We finally arrive at a very nice house. There are other vehicles here but Jeanette tells me, "It's cool, don't worry, we are good," as she parks the Vette. My eyes are searching for any dogs or people that may be lurking in the shadows. The area seems to be clear.

We walk into a very nice home. The entry is a great atrium area with lots of glass. Jeanette brings me past the kitchen and dining area into a large living room, I mean large living room area.

All of a sudden she just starts running and turns down a hallway, I start to follow, thinking it's a game. I chase her down one long hallway before we get to a corner. She turns the corner and keeps running. As I come around the corner, I see a door at the end of the hall being closed.

The echo is loud enough to make me stop, jump back and return to the living room area.

I sit down on the couch, my head in my hands. Okay, what am I going to do in this scenario, I keep asking myself. Okay, just be calm and find a bathroom first. When all else fails, always ask to use the bathroom. It works, try it.

I get up and walk back toward the kitchen area to stay away from what looked like multiple bedrooms at the other end of the house and I luck out—a small bathroom off the kitchen like any upscale home should have.

Me being me, I decide, "Let's do it, I'm going to search the whole house." I look at myself in the bathroom mirror, and when I turn around I see a clock on a shelf that says 12:22 p.m. I have no weapons on me. Just be cool and relaxed, open every door and see who the hell is in this house besides me.

I'm sick of being treated like this every time a woman gets sweet on me, being abandoned or chased off by third-party intrusions. Time to get into the game all the way, let's figure this one out if possible, what's the game tonight in Anchorage, Alaska, who's hunting who.

I just walked back through the living room area and haven't seen anyone. As I'm walking down the main hallway, the first door comes up on my left; I stop and open it. There's what looks like one woman sleeping on a smaller twin-sized bed. I step right over to confirm, and yes, this is a lady, she is snoring lightly, looking right at me but her eyes are closed tight in sleep.

I step back out into the hallway and close her door. The next door is about ten steps on my right side this time. I stop and open the door, look in, and I can see three kids all sleeping on a very big bed—no need to go into this room, I can clearly see who is in it; don't want to scare any kids tonight, bad energy.

The next door is right across the hall—three steps and I am at it. I slowly open this door but I can't see the bed. I actually have to walk all the way in and turn a corner to find this bed.

There is a young couple sleeping, a man and a woman sleeping together in this bed. They are facing each other, sleeping on their sides, both snoring lightly. I back quietly out into the hallway in my quest for information, intelligence gathering, data collection, call it what you want.

I come out and walk around the corner of the main hallway. I am starting to walk toward the door at the end, that's the door I last saw Jeanette go into.

I pass a laundry area on my right and another bathroom. I can see one more door over on my left so I walk over and open it up. There is an older couple sleeping together on a midsized bed. The lady is snoring very loudly and I almost laugh.

I am starting to creep myself out with what I am doing but I only have one more door to go. Just hang in there, I tell myself.

I walk over to the door Jeanette went into and I open the door right up, again it's a larger room and I can't see the bed area clearly so I have to walk in. I can hear snoring as I approach the bed, and sure enough, it's her, it's Jeanette.

Oh, but Jeanette is not alone tonight, not my luck, not with another woman either, guess that fantasy can wait also. I can see she is sleeping with a guy—they are entangled in arms and legs, they are together for sure, sharing love with each other at least for tonight.

Well, I searched the whole house going room to room looking for my treasure, behind every door I looked, no heart of gold did I ever find. My heart has been crushed again like glass, shattered by night shadows that hold others tight, me they keep pushing away.

I walk back through the silent house alone, a stranger in someone else's home, a stranger in another land searching for that pulsing heartbeat of eternal love.

I walk over into the kitchen area and start searching by the telephone for a phone number. I need a taxi right now to whisk me away into the deepening night. I see a little sticker that says Checker Cab. Nice, I am in luck. I grab the phone and dial their number.

Dispatch explains to me that she can have a driver meet me at Wyoming Dr and W.36th Ave in about twenty minutes. Yes please, I order the ride up.

There's a pencil and pad of writing paper next to it near the telephone, I decide to write Jeanette a thank you note for all her Alaskan hospitality. "Jeanette, you have been a great host. I appreciate all your humor. As a stranger into the night I go, my friend."

As I am leaving, I make sure the door is locked and secured behind me. I want to make sure I help protect my new friends as they soundly sleep through the night. Wishing them sweet dreams, I walk down their front steps into the gripping cold of the night.

When I get to the meeting spot, there's a taxi already sitting at the curb waiting for me. The driver's side window is down. I can see an arm holding a cigarette out the window. As I am getting in, the guy driving apologizes for the cigarette smoke, tells me he hopes I am ok with it. I tell him to get me as close to Fort Richardson as possible, hopefully the front gate area.

He drives down Wyoming Dr to Spenard Rd, takes the left onto Spenard. The driver looks over at me and says, "Looks like you got some tonight."

I respond to him, "When you say got some, what are you referring to exactly?"

The guy is staring straight ahead driving when he starts to speak to me again, "I was up on the slopes for nine months last summer, came home and my wife gave me a raging case of gonorrhea." I put my face against my hand and lean it into the window trying to lose the sound of his voice.

He continues, "Yeah, now she took off with the other guy to Texas and they took my three daughters with them. She stole everything I owned except my clothes."

I am asking myself this question right now in my mind as he talks, *Is every taxi driver in Anchorage this dysfunctional? Is it Anchorage, is it me, is it all of us together?*

Collaborative dysfunction, I think to myself.

I start laughing and the guy stops mid-sentence. He must think I am laughing at him. I keep my thoughts to myself but he stops talking.

Sweet silence looking out the window, tame the wild beast that is your emotional rage surging up inside of you, people pushing their emotional poison on me everywhere I go.

Maybe someday I will buy a little place over near downtown Anchorage, I can offer couches and an open ear. I will have it divided into a girl's side and guy's side, both sides separated by barbed wire. I will name it "Courts of Chaos," caution to all whom choose to enter.

Chapter 13

I Know That Face

Mid-March 1983, I am fourteen days short. In military jargon that means I leave Alaska in two weeks. I start the clearing process ten days from now in preparation for my departure.

The 172nd Infantry Brigade has just returned from "BrimFrost 82-83," a large multinational, joint force, live fire training exercise that lasted for ninety-six days. We expended large amounts of munitions during BrimFrost. The ground shook for fifteen days straight at one point, very thick smoke blinding us day and night, welcoming us to hell.

Time for me to go downtown Anchorage to see some people, maybe for the last time. I get on a People Mover bus in front of the Enlisted Members Club on Fort Richardson and decide to get off at the bus station on W.6th Ave.

I am going to walk the three-and-a-half blocks over to JC Penney and go up into their bridge over W.6th Ave. I like standing there watching the traffic. It's become a comical distraction for me.

It's cold this evening and there are plenty of people out shopping. The crowds of people surprise me for some reason, so I decide to cut my visit on the bridge short. I walk through the store and exit out the door over on W.5th Ave.

I walk across to D St, then walk up to and into 417 D St. Snoopy's TeeShirt Shop and Video Arcade, where I stop in and talk with my friend Eddie Roach. I hang out here for some time until I start to get hungry, I ask Roach if he can close the store early to go and eat—he can't tonight. Not tonight, he says.

We shake hands. I promise to call him soon. He tells me I better call, and laughs with me. Roach turns to me and says, "Little Brother, good seeing ya, be good out here tonight, ok man?"

"Peace, brother," I respond as I walk out.

I'm heading over to Club Paris to eat. It's an easy stroll from Snoopy's. When I get there, even though I am alone, the atmosphere is inviting. As I step in, laughter echoes out onto the sidewalk past me like a wave.

Their best bartender is on tonight. This guy makes the best frozen White Russians in Anchorage. He has a ritual every time he comes in for work. He smiles as he comes in, saying hello to everyone he walks past, then he goes over behind the bar and removes his street jacket and hangs it up on a hook.

Sometimes he carries a dry cleaned garment bag with him that has his bartender's vest, sometimes the vest is already hanging behind the bar.

When he puts the vest on, he looks right at people as he is buttoning it up, smiling, big mustache always neatly trimmed. When you run up a tab, he throws you a free drink after every fifth drink. He is raking the tips back in, that's for sure.

I get a pleasant surprise when two ladies from Germany approach me and offer to buy me a shot of whiskey. We talk for a while. I love their accents.

It's 6:35 p.m. when I finally get a table. I prefer not eating in a bar area, so the wait is worth it for me. I order the snow crab legs with another frozen White Russian. With a huge grin, my waitress tells me my order is sexy. Be right back with rolls, she says.

It's seeming to me that we are flirting but she is working, part of her job is being friendly, maybe even slightly flirtatious. Possibly pump up her tips if she has the right customers.

As usual, the meal is great tonight. I am asking my waitress for the check when she asks me if she can sit down for a second. I tell her, sure thing. She jumps right into asking me, "Do you need to get slapped tonight?"

Not being sure what she means, I am feeling a little bewildered when it hits me what she is asking me. I lean in a little closer across the table, smiling, when she says, "You need a good slap tonight don't ya honey?"

I am laughing and thinking to myself, *Now, that's an Alaskan happy meal being offered at Club Paris.*

When I am outside, it feels good to start walking again, I decide to walk the length of 4th Ave one more time from L St to at least Juneau St. Let's see who I bump into tonight.

It takes me a while before I get into the area where The Wild Cherry and The Booby Trap exotic dance clubs are. As I walk up on the intersection of E.4th Ave and Cordova St, I can see about ten to fifteen girls standing on the other side of the intersection.

I think I recognize one of them, so I cross the street to see if it's her. Two or three of the girls look my way and all start yelling at once, "It's the Little Brother, it's the Little Brother."

I have three or four girls talking to me frantically all at once.

"Little Brother, help us, there's a weird scary guy offering us $300 to do photo shoots. He won't leave us alone, he keeps driving by then he goes down and pulls onto Denali St and parks for a while, waiting. Help us get rid of him. He won't leave us alone."

"Girls, please, one at a time. What are you saying about $300?" I ask.

One of the girls steps up to speak and tells me, "Little Brother, he pulls up in his pickup truck camper asking if one of us wants to go with him and do a photo shoot for $300. It'll be quick and fun," he says.

Another one of the girls then tells me, "Everyone keeps telling him to get lost but he has been circling for almost an hour now at least."

I've been hearing this nonsense about a $300 photo shoot for almost two years now. Andrea was telling me the guy that offered her $300 was kind of weird also but she thought he was harmless.

I ask all the girls, "Let's go, let's go down and we will all tell him to take off together." I get about five or six of the girls to follow me as we all walk down E.4th Ave toward Denali St. "Let's go see who this guy is," I keep telling the girls as we walk the hundred yards or so to Denali St.

I can't wait to see who this guy is. I have a nice pair of black leather gloves on and it's cold out here. The leather will rip skin like a razor blade. As we turn the corner onto Denali St, I see an older pickup truck with a camper top on it parked facing away from us. I can see it's got a pretty good tilt to the left. The exhaust is making a funny noise as the truck idles.

The driver must see us because his brake lights just came on. I tell the girls to start making snowballs, and we start pegging snowballs at the back of his truck. We start laughing as the driver puts the truck into gear because his tires are spinning and the truck slides sideways into the curb.

I am running up alongside the truck, pounding on the camper until I get to the side of his door. His tires are still spinning on the ice, he's going nowhere slowly. He turns and looks at me with a frantic look on his face while I am pounding on his driver's window.

I am screaming at him, "Get out, you're done. Get out, you're done. Stop the vehicle." He looks at me frantically with fear. I recognize him this time. I know that face, I've seen those glasses.

Suddenly his tires catch some dry pavement and he gets about fifty feet up Denali St before he starts to slow down again, me and one of the girls are still running after him with snowballs in our hands.

The girl with me is dressed in a way I will never be able to forget—she's wearing high heels with pink stockings, a red leather skirt with a blue leather jacket that has long tassels, a white cowboy hat covering her long blonde hair.

We both throw snowballs at the back of the truck, hitting it as he drives off, noisy exhaust and creaky suspension echoing down Denali St, reverberating down that lonely road.

The girl turns and tells me, "Wow, that was intense, Little Brother. Thank you," as we slap hands.

The rest of the girls have now come around the corner and I tell them all to be careful out here, be weary, stay vigilant, I say, as I jump into a taxi that has pulled over.

The taxi driver is a woman and she is talking to me about lost loves. I've been divorced four times, she explains, then goes into detail about her last divorce.

I drown her voice out in my mind by thinking about the guy on Denali St. I know I know that face, I just can't place it. It's haunting me but I know I've seen that guy before.

Several days later I am sitting here on a tarmac at Anchorage International Airport waiting in a commercial plane getting ready to fly south to Seattle.

It's midnight and the night skies are clear. We will have smooth flying, I am told, relax and enjoy the flight, please. I am glad to take a seat at starboard allowing me to see Anchorage one last time tonight.

As my plane pushes up into the Chugach Mountains and does the big turn toward Turnagain Arm, I can see Sleeping Lady through my window. Snow covered, she shines over in the distance through the crystal clear skies.

Sleeping Lady is waving goodbye to me now. She tilts her head back while she laughs, frozen ground stretching out beyond.

ſ

Last Thoughts

Enchantment

I was stationed at Fort Richardson with the 172nd Light Infantry Brigade from 1981 to 1983. A member of the 562nd Engineer Company, 2nd Platoon. I left Alaska in late March 1983. It's now 2013.

I have just finished watching a movie about a prolific serial killer who resided in Alaska. He owned a bakery. His name was Bob Hansen. His most active periods were during 1979–1983. He supposedly has bodies scattered all over southcentral Alaska, his victims of hate all waiting to be found.

During the movie, On Frozen Ground, the intense emotional feelings that kept washing over me, that this was all just so very familiar, were overwhelming for me.

During the end credits, they started showing the real-life pictures is when I realized what I had been a peripheral part of, something so much bigger than me, myself being a secondary character at the very best, tertiary even.

I recognized Hansen immediately from the bakery interview back in 1981, but it hit me it was also him whom I ran into during my last night in downtown Anchorage on Denali St. It was Bob, the owner in that truck. Chills are running through my body; I feel paralyzed with emotion.

Then I see her face, Andrea Mona Altiery. My body goes limp. I start sobbing when I realize he got her. Andrea was a beautiful exotic dancer that used the stage name Enchantment.

That degenerate animal killed Andrea. I had my hands on him, shook his hand, punched on his truck, threw snowballs at him, and looked right into his eyes. All along, he knew where they were all at, hiding them from our view.

I felt like a naive lamb led to his slaughter. I ate food from his bakery, drank his milk, smiled at him. It's a complete and absolute feeling of emptiness, like my whole being has been vacuumed clean.

I start to imagine the helplessness, the complete feeling, of being alone these women had. Andrea must have had while being preyed upon all of their spirits gathering together now. None of these women deserved to have been dehumanized like this and erased from our minds.

Most of them ventured to the last frontier from somewhere else, not fully understanding where they had found themselves because it was a land full of strangers. Each woman called it home, and for the moment, they were. Andrea Altiery's reality is different now. She's dancing in her grave with all the other enchanted spirits. Each woman has been calling out to us, asking to be remembered, begging us to listen.